TECHSHIELD CAMP

Where Kids Learn to Keep the Internet Safe!

BY ELIZABETH SULLIVAN

As the sun peeked over the horizon, casting a golden glow over the building of TechShield camp, Keanu, Kaitlin, Jeremy, and Suze walked in together, excited for the week of cybersecurity camp ahead.

Once inside, they stood at the entrance, their eyes wide with excitement.

"Whoa, check out this place!" Keanu exclaimed, scanning the room with anticipation.

Suze took in the scene with a thoughtful expression. "I wonder what kind of challenges they'll give us".

"I heard we get to learn about blockchain and stuff," Kaitlin added, her voice filled with enthusiasm.

Jeremy nodded, his eyes shining. "Yeah, and test our cybersecurity skills too! It's gonna be awesome!"

As they entered the camp, they were greeted by Professor Code, a lively character with a passion for all things tech.

"Welcome, campers!" he exclaimed, his voice full of energy. "I'm Professor Code, your guide to the world of blockchain and cybersecurity here at TechShield camp. Get ready for the adventure of a lifetime!"

They gathered in a classroom to hear the first assignment. "Your first challenge will be the "Blockchain Fort Challenge," where each team has to design and build their own cybersecurity strategy for a blockchain network".

"You will be put on the Red Team or the Blue Team based on the skills and interests you submitted to camp".

"The Red Team's goal is to attack and breach the defenses of the Blue Team's fort, while the Blue Team will work to protect their network".

Jeremy and Suze were assigned to
the Blue Team.
"This is gonna be so cool," Jeremy said, rubbing
his hands together eagerly.
Suze nodded, with a determined expression.
"Let's show them what we're made of!"

Keanu and Kaitlin found themselves on the
Red Team.
"I can't wait to get started!" Kaitlin exclaimed,
her eyes sparkling with excitement.

As they began building their strategies, the campers dove into the world of blockchain technology, learning more about distributed ledgers, hashing, and cryptography.

They discovered that a distributed ledger meant everyone had a copy of the same information, making it trustworthy and transparent. Hashing turned information into a special string of numbers and letters, like a digital signature. And Cryptography was the art of encoding messages, so only those with the key could read them.

Keanu and Kaitlin were both competitive, and spent the day brainstorming strategies to penetrate the Blue Team's defenses. "We've got to think like hackers," Keanu said, deep in concentration.

Meanwhile, Jeremy and Suze went to work strengthening their fort, and putting security measures in place to protect from any potential attacks. "We need to stay one step ahead," Jeremy said, adjusting the firewall settings with precision. "I feel confident in our incident response plan" said Suze.

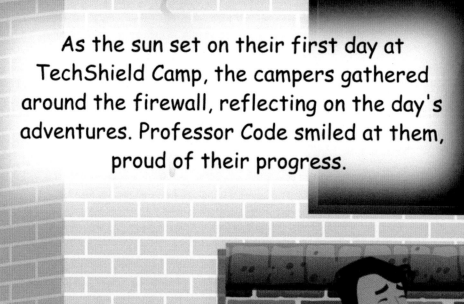

As the sun set on their first day at TechShield Camp, the campers gathered around the firewall, reflecting on the day's adventures. Professor Code smiled at them, proud of their progress.

"You've all done an amazing job today," he said. "Blue team, tomorrow, we'll see how your fort holds up to the Red Team's attack!"

Excitement buzzed in the air as the campers settled in for the night, eager to see what challenges lay ahead.

The next morning, the campers awoke to the sound of clicking keys and the smell of breakfast burritos being served, a camp favorite. They gathered in the community room, where Professor Code announced the day's challenge.

Today, you'll put your skills to the test in the ultimate showdown between the Red Team and the Blue Team," he explained, eyes darting across the screen of his laptop. "The Red Team will launch a simulated cyber-attack on the Blue Team's fort, while the Blue Team defends."

Keanu and Kaitlin, ready for action, huddled together to finalize their attack strategy. "We need to perform reconnaissance and scan for open ports and vulnerabilities," Keanu said, his eyes gleaming with determination.

Jeremy and Suze, on the Blue Team, stood side by side, ready to defend their fort at all costs. "We'll set up intrusion detection systems and implement access control measures," Jeremy said, giving Suze a reassuring nod.

As the attack began, Keanu and Kaitlin used social engineering tactics to trick the Blue Team into revealing sensitive information. It worked! The link was clicked on and now they had access to the information they needed. Then they attempted to exploit vulnerabilities in the smart contracts of the Blue Team's network.

Jeremy and Suze sprang into action, responding to the Red Team's attacks with swift precision. They monitored their network traffic using packet sniffers, deployed security patches, and implemented firewall rules to protect their fort.

After hours of intense back-and-forth, the attack finally came to an end. Professor Code gathered the campers to announce the results.

"Wow! Incredible work, campers," he said, a smile spreading across his face. "Both teams showed exceptional skill in cryptography and encryption methods, as well as a solid display of teamwork. But in the end, there can only be one winner."

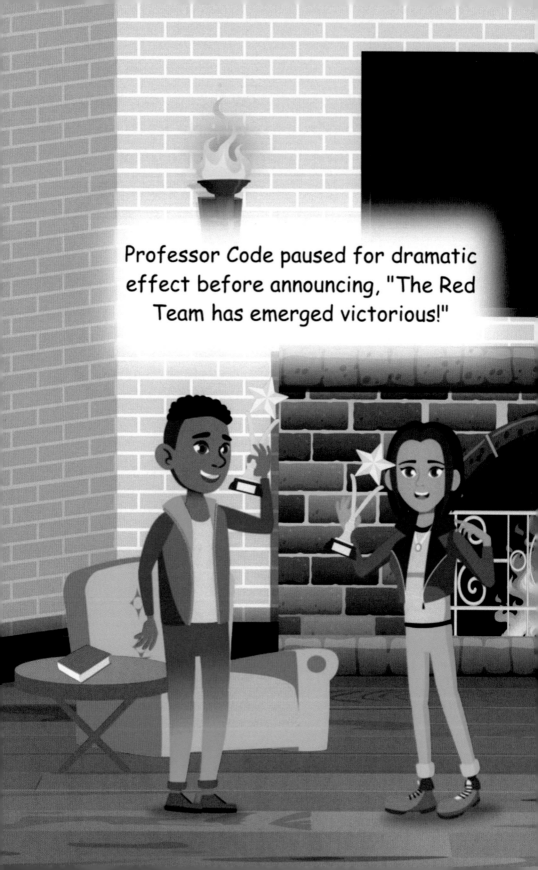

Professor Code paused for dramatic effect before announcing, "The Red Team has emerged victorious!"

The camp erupted into cheers. Keanu high fived Kaitlin. "We make a great team!" Kaitlin said. "You have great hacker skills!" Keanu replied. They cheered celebrating their hard-earned victory.

As the sun set on Techshield Camp, the campers gathered to reflect on their week.

"We came here as individuals, but we leave as a team," Suze said, looking around at her fellow campers. They had learned valuable lessons about cybersecurity, teamwork, and perseverance.

Professor Code stepped forward with a twinkle in his eye. "But the journey doesn't end here," he said. "For those ready to take their skills to the next level, there's Team Purple."

The campers exchanged excited glances. Purple was the ultimate goal, a blend of all the skills combined! One day, they would join the ranks of Team Purple. They were determined.

And with that, the adventure continued, with the promise of new challenges and adventures waiting for them in the world of cybersecurity.

Understanding Cybersecurity: Key Terms from TechShield Camp

Welcome to the world of cybersecurity! Here's a list of important terms you learned about during your adventure at TechShield Camp. Let's explore what each one means:

1. **Cybersecurity**: This is all about protecting computers, networks, and data from bad guys who want to steal or damage them. Think of it as a digital shield for your information.

2. **Blockchain**: A special kind of database that stores information in blocks. Each block is linked to the one before it, making a chain. It's super secure because once a block is added, it can't be changed.

3. **Cryptography**: This is like a secret code. It's a way of writing messages so only the right people can read them. It keeps information safe from hackers.

4. **Distributed Ledger**: Imagine a notebook that everyone can see and write in. A distributed ledger is like that but on computers. Everyone has a copy, so it's really hard to cheat.

5. **Hashing**: This is a way to turn information into a unique string of letters and numbers. It's like creating a fingerprint for data. Even a small change in the data makes a big change in the hash.

6. **Consensus Algorithms**: These are rules for making sure everyone agrees on the data in a blockchain. It's like having a vote to make sure everything is correct.

7. **Smart Contracts**: These are computer programs that automatically do things when certain conditions are met. Think of them like digital promises that can't be broken.

8. **Red Team**: In cybersecurity, the Red Team pretends to be the bad guys. They try to hack into systems to find weak spots before real hackers can.

9. **Blue Team**: The Blue Team defends against attacks. They set up security measures to protect systems and respond to threats.

10. **Reconnaissance**: This is the first step in hacking where you gather information about your target. It's like spying to find out what you're up against.

11. **Vulnerabilities**: These are weak spots in a system that hackers can exploit. Finding and fixing them is really important to keep things safe.

12. **Social Engineering**: This is a trick hackers use to fool people into giving away secrets. It might be a fake email that looks real, asking for your password.

13. **Intrusion Detection Systems (IDS)**: These are tools that watch over a network and alert you if they spot anything suspicious, like a digital security guard.

14. **Access Control Measures**: These are rules that decide who can see or use information. It's like having a key to a locked door—only the right people can get in.

15. **Packet Sniffers**: These tools capture data traveling over a network. It's like eavesdropping on digital conversations to spot any bad activity.

16. **Security Patches**: These are updates that fix problems in software. Installing them is like repairing a hole in a fence to keep intruders out.

17. **Firewall**: A firewall is a barrier that protects a computer or network from bad guys. It decides what traffic can pass through based on security rules.

18. **Incident Response Plan**: This is a plan for what to do if there's a security breach. It's like having a fire drill so everyone knows how to stay safe.

19. **Team Purple**: The next level of cybersecurity, combining the skills of both Red and Blue Teams. They understand how to attack and defend, making them very powerful protectors.

By learning these terms, you're on your way to becoming a cybersecurity expert, just like the campers at TechShield Camp! Keep exploring and stay curious—the digital world is full of exciting challenges and adventures!

Keep Exploring!

Remember, the skills you learn today can help you keep yourself and others safe online. Keep practicing, stay curious, and never stop exploring the exciting possibilities of technology and cybersecurity. Who knows? One day, you might even become a member of Team Purple.

If you enjoyed this, there's more!

Books can be found at
www.WAGMIConsultingGroup.com

Made in the USA
Middletown, DE
07 July 2024

56984327R00022